Grandma's Silent Auction
June
BY: Michael James

Copyright © 2020 by Michael James

All rights reserved.

No part of this book may be reproduced in any form or by any electronic or mechanical means, including information storage and retrieval systems, without written permission from the author, except for the use of brief quotations in a book review.

CHAPTER ONE
CIARA

Arriving at the airport, I start looking for the lounge right away. My spirits were greatly lifted by one simple email. I am so happy that I can't wipe the smile off my face. As I pass by a restroom, I think to myself I should freshen up, so I turn back around. I left Seven Jewels without checking to see if I looked presentable. I would hate to look like a hot mess after the awkward goodbye with Gaetano.

I notice a few spots where my eyeliner smudged so I use my finger to blend it in the best I can. I finger comb my hair instead of digging through my luggage to find a brush. I am not looking my best, but I am not looking my worst either.

I exit the restroom with a smile on my face and continue searching for the lounge. Since I've only been to this particular airport once, I really have no idea where I'm going. I might as well stop at the information desk and ask. I'm sure it would save me time and a lot of aggravation. This airport is quite busy.

I'm waiting in line and I see someone who looks familiar to me. I get up on my tiptoes to see better. Oh my God!

I get out of line and start walking in their direction and yell out, *"Martha, Shay."* I get no response so I walk faster. *"Martha, Shay,"* I repeat but a tad bit louder.

Shay turns at the sound of her name. *"Ciara,"* she says with so much excitement in her tiny voice.

Martha now looks and both seem thrilled to see me. They begin to come toward me and I pick up my pace to them. I hug Shay as soon she's right in front of me.

"How are you?"
"I'm good! I've missed you. Daddy has too."
"Yeah? I miss you as well."

I step back and say hello to Martha and she does the same.

"Is Warrick with you two?"
"Daddy had to leave and we are going home."
"Ahh, I see."

Martha checks the time on her watch. *"We only*

have a few minutes to get to our flight. Are you heading back to New York?"

"I am, but not on this flight. It was all booked."

"That stinks!" Shay says.

"I agree. It would have been nice to see you longer."

"Maybe you can come over?"

"I'll try, but I can't guarantee anything. I won't be home very long."

Shay throws herself into my body and I wrap my arms around her, giving her a hug.

"I'm sorry, but we really have to go."

I watch as the two of them walk away. Seeing her with a frown really hurts my heart. She's such a sweet little girl. She looks tired. It is awfully late for her to be up.

When I get my bearings I remember what I'm doing here. When I turn back to go to the information desk, I catch a sign for the lounge. That saved me a bit of time.

The lounge isn't overly crowded, so it's easy to see that I am the first one here. I pick a table and set my belongings to the side out of the way. After I have a seat, I dig into my purse for my phone.

"Is this seat taken?"

My lips instantly curled into a smile before I

could lift my head. I know that voice even though it's been a while since I heard it.

Jumping out of my seat, I leap right into his arms. I just about knock him over, but he manages to stabilize us.

"God, I've waited so long to feel you in my arms again." His words are soft next to my ear.

I lean my head back to see his handsome face. He cups both sides of my face and plants his lips on mine. It feels like the first kiss all over again. I melt all over again, as well.

"Hi!"

"Hi!"

"How long do you have before your flight?"

"Little less than two hours."

"How did you know I was in Vegas?"

"Gotta love the tabloids!"

"Oh! Those people won't leave me alone."

"How long do you have?"

"A little longer than you."

"Do you want a drink or maybe go for a walk?"

"Whatever you want to do, I'm good with it."

One of his eyebrows arched and I giggled. His eyes travel all over my face as if there's a road map printed on it. I search his eyes and I see he hasn't lost feelings for me. That makes my smile even bigger.

"Let's go for a walk," he finally says.

The feeling of his hand in mine is a reminder that this man loves me and I fell in love with him. I wasn't sure until now if my feelings were fading as time went on. It's encouraging to know that they are not going anywhere.

We get outside and we get into a cab. There is a park not too far from here. We decided to go there because we really just want alone time. If the tabloids catch us, Grams and all the other guys will know I broke a rule. I highly doubt they will be around at this hour.

"I was interviewed by Jacquelyn in April."

"You were?"

"I was. How come you haven't been in contact with her yet?"

"I don't feel I need to justify my life to anyone. The tabloids and the people who read it don't care about the truth."

"Fair enough."

When we reach the park we drag our luggage behind us through the park. I bet we look a little ridiculous, but it's worth it to have this little bit of time with him.

We find a park bench that is under a blooming dogwood tree. The outdoor lighting gives it just enough light to see it. It's beautiful to see, but not as gorgeous as the man sitting next to me. I have truly missed being with him. It makes me wonder if I'd feel the same way if I were with any one of the other guys. I'm not naive enough to know feelings can fade with time and new relationships develop.

"I want to know everything you've been doing lately."

"It's not really all that interesting. I've been doing a lot of traveling as you already know. I'm looking forward to going home. I'm taking a week off when I get home. I'll be seeing my family whom I have not seen in quite some time."

"That should be nice. I bet they are thrilled you're going home."

"Very! They have a family picnic planned for tomorrow. I wish you could come with me."

"Yeah, that would be nice."

"You could come with me. I can buy you a ticket."

"I wish! I actually do need to go home. I told Porter I'd be back. I have a designer dress that I have to do in a day. I know Grams told me I couldn't work this year, but this is a special occasion."

"What's it for?"

"One of Porter's younger cousin's is cancer-free,

CHAPTER 1

and the parents are throwing her a ball next week, so I told him I'd make a gown for her to wear."

"That's very sweet of you." He tucks my hair behind my ear as a light breeze keeps blowing it in my face. *"You know the tabloids are wrong about you. You are one of the kindest and caring people I know."*

I lean into his space and put my arms around his neck and kiss him. We get lost in the moment for a bit. I can't help but wish we didn't have to say goodbye again.

"Thank you for saying that."

"I better get heading back. If I miss my flight, my mom will not be too happy with me."

It's been an hour already? I wish the hour wasn't so short. It feels like it's only been five minutes.

On our way back in the backseat of the cab, his hand was holding mine the entire time. We kept giving each other sweet little kisses. I didn't want this time to end. I wish I could go home with him, but I know I can't. It saddens me that I won't see him again until November. It breaks my heart watching him board a plane without me.

CHAPTER TWO
CIARA

My flight home was relaxing once I got into the air. I'm still not getting used to the take-off. With how much I've been on a plane lately, you'd think my fears would subside but they haven't. Maybe it's just something I'll never be comfortable with.

The end of March was the last time I was home. I was so excited to walk through the door of my apartment. But I was also exhausted. I've been up for the last twenty hours. I dropped my luggage at the door, took a quick shower, and went right to bed. I was out within minutes.

It was almost noon by the time I crawled out of bed. I called Porter as soon as I made some hot tea. It only takes him about fifteen minutes to get here, so he should be here any minute. I am looking forward to getting my hands on Alaska. A certain someone asked me to send a picture of her once I am with her again.

My little puppy, I'm sure has grown, but I hope not too much. She also better remember who I am. It might crush me a bit if she doesn't.

I do a little happy dance when there's a knock on the door. Porter catches me in my glory since he never waits for me to answer the door. I go running and steal Alaska from his arms, giving her lots of kisses. My reward is licking all over my cheek.

"Daddy says he needs a picture of you."

"Looks like someone missed you!"

"I missed her, too."

Porter and I go into the living room and sit on the couch together. I get my phone and snap a picture of me with Alaska. I send it off to Malcolm.

I glance at Porter. *"What?"*

"Rule-breaking I see."

"Yep, guilty as accused."

"How long have you been in contact with Malcolm?"

"Today wasn't the first time."

"Ciara! Do spill."

"I've been keeping in contact with him. I've also talked with Hawk, Warrick, and Kaiden."

"Girl, your grandma finds out she might not be too happy with you."

"It's only been texting, emails, or phone calls until today."

"What is that supposed to mean?"

"I saw Malcolm today... at the airport."

"And?"

I smile. I think about teasing him a little. *"It was amazing."* Okay, the teasing didn't work out so hot. I'm too happy to contain my excitement.

"So, you like him?"

"Like him? I love him."

"Is he the one for you?"

I shrug my shoulders. *"He's not the only one I have feelings for."*

"Who else?"

"Maybe all of them."

Both his eyebrows rise. *"You are so in trouble. You can't really love five guys! How the hell are you going to pick?"*

"Good question. I'll figure it out, right?"

"I don't want to be a downer, but you might want to start figuring your feelings out sooner rather than later."

"And how do you suggest I do that? I'm not even done meeting men!"

CHAPTER 2

"I don't really know." Porter runs a hand through his hair. *"Please don't take what I'm going to say the wrong way."*

"Porter, you are my best friend. We've known each other for a long time, and I know you would never steer me wrong."

"Your choice in men hasn't always been good. I know these men Millie hooked you up with are decent men. Any one of them would probably be the right guy for you."

"But?"

"They are treating you the way you always should have been treated. At some point, you have to figure out if they are in a friend zone or life-long partner zone."

"I don't fully understand what you are getting at. I love these guys for different reasons and qualities."

"Who gives you butterflies and who do you think about the second you wake up every day?"

I don't think Porter understands, I'm in love with more than one man. If he were in my shoes, he would get that my heart is split into pieces and each man has a place in it. I could see myself marrying any one of them.

"I know in my head you are right. My heart doesn't know where it belongs, yet."

"I think you'll figure it out. I just don't think you should wait until November to start weeding some of these guys out of the equation."

I know he's right, I just don't want him to be right. *"I'm just going to marry them all,"* I say as a joke.

Porter starts to laugh. *"I'll call you the traveling wife. Every ten weeks you'll be with husband number one. The tabloids would have a field day."*

"I'll just move them all into Grams mansion. Problem solved."

We both bust up laughing.

When the laughter stops I am glad about the subject change. Porter asked me what material I plan on using to make his cousin's gown with. It's been so long since I've been in my store, so we went downstairs to look. I want him to help me pick it out since he should have an idea of her style and colors she might like.

Porter and I go through a lot of material just to end up with the first one that was picked. The background is black and it has purple and pink flowers better spaced out so that it isn't overwhelming with flowers. I agreed right away with his choice but he wanted to see what else I had. Sometimes your first instinct is all you need.

CHAPTER 2

I was going to let Porter pick out a pattern, but I figured it would just hold up the time that I have to make this dress. So instead, we ordered lunch and I decided that the dress was going to be a surprise to him.

After we had lunch and had more conversations about the guys, before I kicked him out. If I didn't kick him out I would never get this dress made in time. I only have twelve hours before I have to get ready to go off to upstate New York to meet Mr. June. I haven't really decided if I'm excited to meet Lincoln Titus, or if I really just don't wanna deal with it. Through the conversation that Porter and I had during lunch, I have a good idea where my heart lies. Although, I am still unsure of my own decision. I know that I still have a lot of time to make such an important choice, and I'm not sure if I am ready to shut the door on possibly the man of my dreams because I may not have found him yet. However, I am pretty confident about what I thought about today. I am finding that true love isn't an easy choice when I have met all these amazing men. It's hard to believe before Grams' silent auction I was ready to settle on such a bad relationship. Hunter was all wrong for me. He clearly had no regard for me. He needs a kick in the ass and needs to learn how to treat a lady. I think I owe Grams a big thank you for showing me I deserved better. I just wish she didn't make my choices this difficult. Now that Porter is gone, I am getting into my own head again. I thought making this dress would keep my mind from wandering, but it hasn't. I think my heart is still undecided. Any one of the next five guys could steal my heart completely from the first five. This is the part where I wish Grams didn't give me so many wonderful choices.

CHAPTER THREE
CIARA

It took me six hours to make the dress for Porter's cousin. I have to say, I think she and Porter will both love it. I won't be here to see her reaction, but I'll get to see Porter in about fifteen minutes. He is on his way over to get Alaska and the dress. I think I'm going to ask him to go with me to the airport.

I tried calling Grams this morning so that I could swing by to see her, but she didn't answer. It's been far too long since we've seen each other and I am missing our tea together. We haven't gone this long without seeing each other, ever. It's starting to feel strange.

I left myself plenty of time to pack for the next month. I decided to pack lightly since these men think I don't have enough clothes of my own. I packed what I needed for a couple of weeks. I am hoping that Lincoln skips the whole shopping thing. My bedroom is overstuffed with clothes and luggage. If I end up needing something, I'm sure I can find a mall or just do laundry.

Since I had so much time on my hands, I went through my closet and set aside things I don't want anymore, never going to wear, and what was I thinking when I bought those clothes. I bagged them all for donation. I'm sure they will be someone else's treasure. After I did all that, I took a catnap. Nothing like having a good hour-long power nap!

I am startled when Porter excitedly enters my apartment. I might've been lost in thought thinking about my shower. Before I got a hold of Porter to come over, I noticed a text message on my phone from Kaiden. I didn't bother with texting him back. I called him instead. When he asked me what I was doing and I told him I was about to shower, he told me he wanted to watch. I felt very rebellious when I hung up and called him on FaceTime. I propped my phone up where he could see me and also where my phone wouldn't get wet. I don't think I've ever had a hotter shower in my life. Come to think of it, I've never gotten myself off in the shower before. It was a bold move for me. I am starting to like this new bold girl I've become. Having Kaiden telling me where to touch myself was an experience I wouldn't mind having again. Many more times if I'm being completely honest.

"Oh, do tell me what you were daydreaming about!"

I laugh. *"Not going to happen. Every girl has a secret or two that they keep to themselves."*

"That is not fun!"

"Wanna go down to the store and get the dress? I think you're going to love it!"

"I do! I'm sure I will, Ciara because you are the best designer I know."

I smile. *"Thanks!"*

Alaska is curled up on the couch passed out, so I leave her be. Meanwhile, Porter is out the door not even bothering waiting for me to slip my flip flops on. I guess he's a tad bit excited to see the dress. He's got a surprise coming to him because I hid it on him as a joke! This is going to make me laugh. I hope I can keep a straight face.

Porter is unlocking the entrance by the time I catch up to him. I follow him to the backroom, where he thinks the dress is. I can hardly contain my laughter when he unzips the garment bag and sees that it is not the dress that I told him I was making. The gown in the bag is a one-piece. The one I did for his cousin is a two-piece. It's not even the same material. He spins around on his heels faster than I have ever seen him do.

"You changed styles and color?"

"Yeah, the other material wasn't working for me. Were you even sure she'd like a two-piece? Some girls don't like their mid-section showing." I can see the disappointment on his face. *"Take it out of the bag and see it before you judge."*

He takes the dress out and holds it up in front of himself. I watch his expression change. He knows I made this gown months and months ago. *"This is lovely. I hate to ask this because I know you so well, but did you fuck up the one you were making for her? This one you made last October."*

"Well, you know the secret I have? It might have distracted me and left me no time to design a new gown."

I laugh when he wiggles his eyebrows. *"What did you do?"*

"I might have had phone sex with someone instead."

His eyes get big. *"How much phone sex did you have to last hours?"*

"It was at least a good hour. Then we talked and we sort kept going back to phone sex. Have you ever

done that? It's incredible and my god does it get hot. Even when in a cool shower."

"I'm sure she'll love the dress."

I almost burst out laughing. I am glad he wasn't looking at me. If he had, my whole joke would have been ruined.

"It's the right size, right?"

"It looks right!"

"Oh, you know what? She's going to need a strapless bra. We should get her one."

"Good idea."

"Why don't you go and pick one out. I'll put the gown back in the bag."

When Porter is out of the backroom, I sneak over to watch him from the doorway. He's going to flip when he realizes I got him good.

"Ciara, I'm going to get you for this!" he says, while practically jumping for joy.

"What do you think?"

"I love it! So will, Helena. Thank you so much!"

"You are welcome!"

"I'm serious. You're the best! I owe you for this."

"Porter, you don't owe me anything. This is what friends are for."

"Does this mean you didn't have phone sex?"

"I'll never tell."

"You naughty little girl. You totally did! I have to say, I'm getting a bit jealous of all the hot sex you're having. I haven't had a date in months."

"I'll tell Grams to hook you up if she ever calls me back today."

"Please do, but two or three is my cut off." He busts out laughing. *"Maybe five."*

We pack up the gown and go back upstairs to my apartment. I get my belongings and say goodbye to Alaska. I changed my mind about having him take me to the airport. I didn't want my puppy to have to wait in the car while he would've wanted to come inside to see me off. It's easier this way. No public goodbyes as bored people watch.

I get buckled into my seat and put my headphones in. Ready or not, here I come upstate. I still have mixed feelings about if I'm looking forward to meeting Lincoln Titus or not. I definitely don't need to fall for another guy, however, I am not going to settle. I want to marry the right guy for me.

CHAPTER FOUR
CIARA

Landing in a small city in upstate New York, I started looking for a person holding a sign with my name on it once I got my luggage. I've heard about this area, but I haven't ever made it here. I almost did once, however, I can't recall exactly where, though. I don't even remember what it was for, either. It was a few years back.

I spot my name on a very nice welcome sign. This lady put effort into making it. It's white card stock with red hearts drawn on it and my name is in black. I think it's sweet she took the time to make such a nice sign. If she did it that is. Maybe Lincoln Titus did it himself. I doubt it though. Most men wouldn't take the time or effort.

I walk right up to her. *"Hello. I'm Ciara."*

"Hello, Ciara, I'm Tracy Leroux, Lincoln's assistant."

"It's nice to meet you. Is he here?"

"He isn't, but you'll be meeting him tomorrow. Today you are stuck with me."

"Okay! Where are we off to? I hope it's not shopping."

"Well, that was on the agenda, but I see you brought luggage."

"Believe me, I have enough clothes."

"How about I take you to the hotel where you'll be staying tonight. We can get you settled and then grab a bite to eat. If you are hungry, that is."

"Sounds good."

There's a car waiting for us when we exit the airport. I figured there would be, these guys are always prepared. I wonder if it's just for me or if this would be a normal routine. They all have been successful men, so I would assume it's normal. Grams always has a car waiting for us whenever we have traveled. Money does that, I guess.

I don't know why Lincoln isn't meeting me today. Something important must have come up because I thought I would be with him today. I could ask Tracy, but I've been waiting for her to tell me. Although, I have learned from the other men I've dated that their assistants don't give much information out. Even Grams' 3-ring binder of them offers no details. It's you go here, meet this person, and their name, that's all I get. I am left pretty much in the dark. Occupation in the least would be nice.

We are in the car close to thirty-five minutes before pulling up in front of a hotel. It looks to be a nice place from the outside. I noticed we took the expressway, so I didn't really see much of the small city I landed in. This hotel is up on a hill all by itself. Tracy and I go inside and get checked-in to the Woodcliff. The bellhop comes to take my baggage up to my suit. I go up with him while she gives me privacy to get settled. I'll meet her at the bar when I'm ready. I am not sure if we'll go out to grab a bite to eat or stay in. Either way is cool with me.

I walk into the suite and damn, it's nice. It's an open floor plan with a small dining area, living space, a kitchenette, and a little bar. I go up the spiral staircase to enter a bedroom with a king-sized bed and to my left is the master bath with a stand-up shower and jacuzzi tub. This place is super nice.

I go back down and check out the view, it overlooks a golf course. I can't wait to check out the rest of this place later. Right now I need to freshen up and change my clothing. If we stay here, I don't think my jean skirt and tank top are appropriate for such an elegant place.

I changed into a sundress that I picked out of my closet. I made it last summer. The material is light and almost see-through. It's light pink in color and pretty revealing in the chest area. When I made it, Porter told me it's more daring than what I tend to wear, probably why it sat in my closet for so long. I am getting there with learning it's okay to dress sexy.

When I went to meet up with Tracy, she asked if I had a gown with me. I told her I did not, she told me I would need two. That piqued my interest a lot because of course, she offered no details as to why. We ended up going to the local mall. It wasn't very easy finding a gown this time of year. You would think it would be with the wedding season about to kick off, but nope we spent hours looking. I finally found two formal dresses and then we went out for an early dinner. The place we went to was right at the mall, I gotta say the burger I had was delicious. It was huge and super juicy. I didn't care for the fries that came with it. I don't really like steak fries. While we enjoyed our meal we also had a drink. I went outside the box and had a local brewed dark beer. It wasn't really my cup of tea. It was worth going there just for the burger alone.

After we ate, I came back to the hotel to relax in my suite. It's been a long day and I plan on making it an early night. I relaxed on the sofa in the living space and checked my phone to see if Grams had called me back, but she hadn't. I tried calling her again, but it went right to voicemail. It's not like her to not return a call from me. I am not worried - yet! But, if this goes on for another day or two, I will be.

After flipping through the channels on the television I decide to go up to the bedroom where I lay on the bed. I have the standup shower in my view and I start thinking about the phone sex I had earlier. I'm not going to lie, it's turning me on. I am tempted to call Kaiden.

I sit up on the bed and remove my dress, then I plop backward on the bed. I feel silly that I want to get myself off again. The more I think about this morning, the more I want to touch myself.

I roll over onto my stomach and bury my face in the pillow, letting out a scream. With how much sex I've had in the past few months I should be satisfied. I shouldn't feel the need for sex, right? I've had more orgasms in the last five months than I ever had with past boyfriends.

I get off the bed and go down to the kitchenette to get a drink. Grabbing bottled water, I lean on the bar while I have a few sips. Getting a drink has done nothing to distract my mind. It keeps going back to the shower.

Taking my water with me back to the second floor, I go into the bathroom and turn the water on in the jacuzzi tub. I get it to the perfect temperature before stripping from my bra and panties. I throw my hair up into a messy bun then get into the tub. Pressing the button for the jets, I lean back to relax. With my eyes close, I can hear his voice telling me to touch my clit. I give in and begin to masturbate. The silly feeling I had moments ago about getting myself off, is long gone. It's replaced with a feeling of satisfaction. I shouldn't feel any shame. Having orgasms makes you feel good. Who cares if I am the one that brings me to climax. It's definitely not the same as having a man do it, but it's working. I'm already getting close to cloud nine.

CHAPTER FIVE
CIARA

I had breakfast out on the patio this morning. It was so nice listening to the birds chirping and having the sun shining on me. It was a very relaxing feel and the food was absolutely delicious. I might have been the only one eating alone, but it didn't bother me in the least. People watching is kind of entertaining.

I went back up to my room to get ready for the day. Tracy told me a lady by the name Lyndse Tennant would be coming to pick me up just before noon. Today is one of the days I need to wear a formal gown. Tracy didn't tell me where I am going, but every time I picked a gown, she said it was too much. To me it's not a ball gown kind of day, it's more business clothing than anything. In fact, I'm not wearing a dress at all. I am wearing a sexy pantsuit.

It's all white and the jacket is the shirt! I love how it's out of my comfort zone. I feel extremely sexy in it. Sexy enough that I took a few selfies in it after I put my hair in a side, low ponytail, and added my white Fedora hat. I might have sent the pictures to a few guys I know.

When it was a quarter of twelve, I decided to wait for this Lyndse lady in the lobby. While I was waiting a man walked up to me and made a comment that the only thing my outfit is missing is a cigar. He then said that it would make a wonderful magazine cover. I was caught off guard by his comments, so I jokingly asked if he had one. The man pulled one out of his shirt pocket. I shocked him when I posed and told him to snap a picture with my phone. I might have taken a picture with him as well. He said I made his day.

I watch as a lady comes in through the automatic doors and goes right to the front desk. I figured she is the lady I'm waiting for, so I head in her direction. Sure enough, I heard her ask for my room.

"Hello, I'm Ciara."

She faces me and her eyes get big. She says, *"Wow!"* Underneath her breath. When she stopped gawking at me she spoke again. *"I'm Lyndse."*

"Are you ready to head out?"

"I am if you are."

Once outside, we get in a waiting Towncar. It isn't until we leave and are on the highway she breaks the silence.

"Sorry about my reaction when I saw you. I think you are stunning and wish I could pull off an outfit such as yours."

"I bet you could! I Don't tend to dress like this, but I have to admit it feels good. I think it takes confidence to wear something like this and I don't tend to have a lot of confidence."

"You sure hide that well."

"Thanks, that's reassuring. Honestly, I think you should try out an outfit like this. You could pull it off easily."

"Thank you for saying that. Someday when I get there I just might."

"Are you allowed to tell me where we are heading or is that still a mystery?"

"I am afraid I'm not allowed to spoil it. From what I've gathered about you, you will absolutely love today. Tracey will be waiting for you once we arrive at our destination. It isn't far, probably only a fifteen-minute drive."

"Well if that doesn't make me curious, nothing

will. Do you know if I'll be meeting with Lincoln today?"

"Yes, I believe he will be there. He's very excited to meet you."

"And how do you know Lincoln?"

"I've worked for him for the last three years. I am sort of Tracey's assistant. That's all I can really tell you until you meet him. If I told you what I do, you would figure out what Lincoln does. I guess it's a big surprise."

"A surprise I don't get."

We arrived at another hotel in the city that I landed in yesterday. I find it a bit odd that I didn't just stay here. However, I do love the Woodcliff, so I'm not complaining. Lyndse and I go inside and Tracy is waiting for us. Lyndse says goodbye and Tracy hands me a pass. I put it around my neck. She then gives me a silk piece of material and she giggles when I raise an eyebrow.

"It's for the surprise. Trust me, I won't let you trip or walk into any doorways."

"Good, because I don't need to be wounded by the time I meet Lincoln."

Once we stop laughing, I cover my eyes with the strap and she leads me to wherever we are going. My heart is racing. I cannot wait to find out what this big surprise is all about. I also cannot wait to meet Lincoln and get that part over. The anxiety usually goes away once I meet the guy I'm to spend a month with.

Tracy guided me to a chair and once my ass is parked, I get to take the blindfold off. I see a runway in front of me. A fashion show! Lyndse was right, it is right up my alley. My smile is big when I look at Tracy.

"This is awesome."

"It gets better. Trust me this is going to be amazing." She sits next to me and glances at her watch. *"Less than five minutes before it begins."*

I take this time to let my eyes roam the room. I have no idea what type of show this is. I know none of my clothing is here because I didn't enter anything. I am still excited to see other designers work, though. As I am taking in the room, I notice it's mostly women. There are a few men, but it's less than five.

I turn my attention to the stage with the announcement. I find it odd the speaker says they will begin with men's tuxedos. The odd part is, that one of the men will accompany us after the show is over. A peek over at Tracey she offers me no details on that announcement. I actually notice a slight smile, but she's trying to hide it. I can only assume that Lincoln is part of the fashion show. I could be wrong because honestly, I have no idea when I am going to meet him.

    I forget all about the announcement when the men start walking the runway. Pretty much the tuxes are your average formal entire. There isn't really much we can do with a tux besides color and whether you wear a vest or a cumber bun, that's really about it, so I pay more attention to the men themselves. I am hoping I can figure out if Lincoln Titus is one of them.

    Once all the men have modeled off the tuxedos, there are only two men that might have looked my way. I couldn't figure out if one of them was Mr. June or not. I am going to be in the dark until we finally meet.

    My eyes stay glued to the stage as wedding dresses are modeled off. These gowns are absolutely gorgeous. One dress, in particular, catches my eye right off the bat. I wish I knew someone getting married because I would highly recommend that dress, even though it isn't one of my own.

    After nearly two hours the show is over, I want to see more. I just love fashion shows. I want to know who made the wedding dress I was eyeing. It's not normal for them to not tell us who the designers are,

CHAPTER 5

so that's weird to me. I might have someone in mind who that one dress would look stunning on.

"Hello," a tender voice says beside me.

"Hello," I reply, trying not to sound startled because I was lost in thought and he caught me off guard.

"I'll be your escort for the rest of the party."

"Oh! I didn't realize there was more!"

"One cannot plan a wedding without taste testing cake."

"Cake, huh? I could go for something sweet."

He offers me his elbow, so I stand from my seat and put my hand on his inner elbow. It is then that I notice Tracy slipped away without me noticing. I am glad I at least got one of the two men who looked my way during the show.

"Did you find a dress you like?"

"I did. One really caught my attention."

"Are you going to bid on it?"

"Bid on it?"

"Silent auction is starting soon."

"Oh, I'm not really in the market for a dress."

"No? Aren't you getting married in December?"

"I..." I look right at him when I stumble on my words, *"how did you know that?"*

"I have my ways." He winks at me, and God it is sexy.

"Do I know you?"

"Not yet!" We stop walking and I glance at the table in front of us. *"You need a good six months to plan the perfect wedding,"* he says.

"I don't think I need invites just yet as I have no idea who I'm marrying."

"Take a look. The thing about weddings is everything must be the way you want it, from the invitation right down to the cake and your grand exit."

"You seem to know a lot about weddings."

"It's sort of my specialty."

"I see." I flip open a book. *"Shouldn't I wait until I have a groom?"*

"No harm in getting a feel for what you like. Let me see your phone."

I give him a questioning look, but hand my cell over to him. He takes it and I see him searching in the Apple store. He hands my phone back and I look at it.

"It's a wedding planner. Everything you need is there. Under the category tab, you make notes of things you like."

"I see."

"Let me know when you find an invitation you

CHAPTER 5

like, I'll show you how to save it. That way when you decide who your Prince Charming is, you show him and then order. Makes everything simple."

"That is very convenient."

"It takes a lot of the stress off. I do highly recommend not waiting until the last minute. As I said, six months is generally a good amount of time to plan."

"Gotcha!"

I pine through the book of invites. There are a few that I like. There are so many to choose from and I can see why it would be hard to decide. However, how would I know the color when I don't even know the wedding colors, yet. I do know whenever I've thought about this day in the past, I've always gone to black and white colors. You can't go wrong with black on women.

I showed him the ones I liked and he showed me how to save it to the app he downloaded on my phone. Later this should save me a bunch of time. When I decide who I'm marrying, I can just show him the options and order right off the app.

We move on to cake toppers, centerpieces for tables, flowers, and then we make it to the silent auction tables. It suddenly hit me, the dress I loved, could be mine. Although I've always wanted Grams or myself to make it. I put a bid in any way. I could always find a bride looking for the perfect dress. I am not going to lie, I bid really low.

After the auction, we started taste-testing food. Most of the food is amazing. I put the ones I like the most in the app. Finally, we made it to the cake. I am not hungry anymore, but it's cake, so I'll make room for it. White chocolate with raspberry filling was absolutely my favorite. I almost don't even care who I marry, my mind is made up, that's the one I want.

"Are you ready to head back to the stage?"

"Is there more to the fashion show?"

"Everything gets modeled off again and the winning bids are announced."

"Oh, I see."

I sit where I sat the first time. My sexy guide leaves me. I look around to see if Tracy or Lyndse might have come back, but I don't see either of them. Women start coming out in the dresses and I'm excited because they are telling who won and also who the designers are. So even if I don't win, I'll know who made the one I liked.

After almost two-hours later the dress I like the most comes out and I am shocked! First I learned I won it, but even more surprising is Grams made it. Once my jaw is off the floor, I scan the room. It is common for the designers to be at a show. I spot her in the back of the room with a huge grin on her face. I shake my head. She got me!

Now that the bridal show is over, I also learn that this is Lincoln Titus' bridal show. Since he didn't have a wedding gown in the show, I assume he must be a wedding planner. I can also assume he was my escort today.

CHAPTER SIX
LINCOLN

I have been planning the bridal show for nearly a year. I am thrilled with the outcome. It's been a fabulous day for my business. I am looking forward to checking the stats on my app later tonight. I would do it now, but I have a lovely lady waiting to officially meet me.

I was Ciara's escort today and not once did I lead on that I'm the guy she's spending the next month with. I was glad she didn't ask my name because I wanted to see the things she likes without her thinking she needed to include me in her thought process. Weddings are mostly surrounded by what the woman wants. After all, it's what they dreamed about from childhood.

I am looking forward to telling Ciara who I am. I had the privilege of spending quite a bit of time with

CHAPTER 6

her today and she has a wonderful personality. She is a gorgeous woman, as well. Holy hell, does she pull off the pantsuit she is wearing very well. When I saw her sitting in the front row, my eyes instantly went to her. I had no idea just how beautiful she was.

At the end of last year, Millie Verbank called me and told me all about her silent auction. At first, I thought she wanted me to place a bid. However, that was not the case. I am Mr. June because Millie wanted me to get Ciara prepared to marry in December. She knew that planning a high profile wedding to go off without a hitch, you don't plan a wedding in a month. I am spending the month with Ciara to help get her motivated, not to date her. I didn't bid to date her, my deal with Millie is I get to be the one planning Ciara's lavish wedding. After seeing her, I wish I was part of this crazy idea of Millie's. I have an entire month, so who knows what might happen. I'm not going to turn down a chance at love if it happens. Wouldn't that be a twist in the grand scheme of things? I'm not going to get my hopes up, though. Two of the things I must do in my career is be a good listener and pick up on body language. I think Ciara is already in love. She might not realize it yet, though. It's got to be tough to figure it out with dating so many men. Although, without her knowing, I still might have a chance with her.

I change out of my tux and opt to wear a long-sleeved, cotton, white shirt with a pair of faded blue jeans. Ciara is definitely going to out dress me with her outfit. Honestly, she should. I mean with how damn sexy she is, why not have wishful eyes upon her.

I come out from backstage, Millie is with Ciara. Just when I couldn't imagine Ciara's smile to be more genuine, she proved me wrong. Her smile is lighting up the room. Seeing her talking with her grandmother, you can tell there is a special bond between the two of them. As crazy as I thought Millie's idea was, it was definitely done out of love. One thing I don't get is why the big rush to get her married? That has been a burning question in my mind since Millie came to me. The only answer I came up with was health issues, but Millie doesn't seem to be ill. I guess it's really none of my business.

"Hello, ladies," I say as I approach them.

"Hello, Lincoln," Millie replies, *"have you officially met my granddaughter, Ciara?"*

"I have not."

I smile at Ciara. She speaks before I do. *"I figured*

you might be the man of the month." She stretches out her hand. *"Hi, Lincoln Titus, I am Ciara."*

"It's a pleasure to meet you."

"I was telling Grams what a lovely bridal show you put on here."

"Thank you, it was a lot of work. I am very pleased with the outcome."

"I have a question for you both. What would have happened if I didn't bid on Millie Verbank's wedding gown?"

Millie snickers and says, *"Someone else would have won."*

"So my bid won fair and square?"

"I didn't say that." There is a hint of laughter in Millie's voice. *"Yes, you won it without cheating. Where is your checkbook?"* Again she has laughter in her voice.

"At home. You kind of know where I live, so catch me later."

"I'm not taking your money. I made this dress for you and only you. I would have been crushed if you didn't pick it. No one else was allowed to bid on it."

Ciara hugs her grandmother. *"Thank you so much, Grams."*

"You are welcome."

I interrupt their little moment. *"Can I take you two ladies to dinner tonight?"*

They both smile at one another and answer in unison. *"Yes!"*

"Perfect. I'll have Tracy make us reservations somewhere."

"Text me when and where. I have a few things I must attend to before dinner." Millie gives Ciara a kiss on the cheek before leaving her and me alone.

"Do you want to go back to your hotel room to relax before dinner? I have a few things to tidy up here, otherwise I'll be free in about a half-hour if you wish to do something."

"If you have things to do, I could go back to the hotel."

"I'd love to hang out with you."

"Well, go and do what you need to do. I'll just go and chill at the bar. I saw earlier that there's an outdoor bar."

"Perfect, I'll come and find you in a bit."

Watching Ciara walking away, I want to stop her! I don't really have anything to do, I just told her that so she didn't feel obligated to spend time with me. It's going to be difficult to pretend that we are dating. Is it fair to all the other guys who actually paid to date her, while I just have a deal with Millie? I'm starting to regret the decision I made already. I am highly attracted to her as I'm sure all the other men have been too. I have seen the tabloids, I see the way that the men look at her. In all fairness, I can see why and I have only known her a few hours.

Since I gave myself a half-hour, I might as well check my app status. This is the first time that I have really tested how well this is going to work. If this is a success, I will be doing more shows in the future. Although, they won't be in my prime season. I'll do them more in the fall. This app was made to make things simpler for the high profile weddings I mostly coordinate. I am known to have pulled off some of the best celebrity weddings in the last eight years. Some of them have been well planned out over a year and some of them have been done in just a month or two. I prefer the ones planned for over a year. It's too much stress on everyone involved otherwise.

Checking my stats, I am very pleased with the results. Many women used it today. I am very excited about the amount of business my partners got today. I see all kinds of sales from cake toppers to cake flavors. Three places actually got booked today for next year's weddings. I think my app is going to take off.

Since I have more time on my hands, I search for

Tracy and Lyndse to give them the good news. Both ladies said it would work while I was doubtful. I'm sure both are going to tell me they told me so. While I am at it, the two of them can help me find a place for a nice dinner and something for Ciara and me to do to pass the time.

CHAPTER SEVEN
CIARA

I pick a table out on the patio that has an umbrella to block the sun. It is sunny and very hot today. I almost wish I told Lincoln to meet me at the hotel so that I could change out of this pantsuit. Especially if we are doing anything outside. I did notice this morning when I was having breakfast on the patio that there is a pool. Maybe Lincoln and I could head back there and lounge around in the sun, then do some swimming to cool off. It is unusual for the temperatures to be this hot in New York this early in June. I am not complaining, I've had enough of the cold temperatures to last me a while. One thing about living in New York, we got all four seasons. Winter is my least favorite one. I don't really care to be cold to the point of my teeth chattering, or wearing multiple layers of clothing. But, I do like a big comfy sweater now and then.

I was pretty impressed with Lincoln's bridal show today. It took me some time to catch on that my grandmother would really like me to get planning a wedding for December. I absolutely love that she made the dress that I had my eye on. However, I am not entirely sure that a December wedding is going to happen. I'm not really in a big hurry to marry. A wedding is a big deal, big commitment, and I want to make sure that whoever I end up with at the end of all this, is absolutely the right man for me. I don't know how I am going to decide that in just a few weeks once November hits.

I think about if I pick Malcolm, there are many months that have passed, and that will continue between when we dated. Although it seems nothing has changed so far and our feelings are still intact, it doesn't necessarily mean feelings won't change over the next few months. What if next month he decides that too much time has passed and he moves on? Or say I even picked Warrick, and he decided that I'm not ready for an instant family. There are so many different scenarios to think about in this process, so I am not sure if a December wedding it's appropriate. The only way that I'm going to know anything for sure is months away. With that and Lincoln telling me that I need a good six months to plan a proper wedding, shouldn't I also have a proper six months with the man of my dreams?

I don't want to disappoint anyone. In reality, I know that I could end up disappointing more than one person. I don't like to hurt people. I know how that feels and it's not a very good feeling. Someday I might sit back and think that this was the adventure of a lifetime. Don't get me wrong, I think it is the adventure of a lifetime as I'm going through it. For now, I just need to stay out of my own head and enjoy the adventure I am on. It just really bothers me that I might be the one to hurt some of these men.

"Looks like I get the pleasure of accompanying the most gorgeous woman in the city for the rest of the evening."

"Oh yeah? Where is she hiding?" I am looking in the crowd for a person. *"Is she the one at the bar in light blue?"*

He snickers. *"Hardly! My eyes are on her as we speak."*

I smile. *"Looks like I get to spend the evening with the most handsome man in the city."*

"I know, you lucky, lucky girl!"

We both laugh. *"So, Mr. Handsome, what is the*

hottest couple in the city going to be doing before dinner with Grams?"

"I thought we could take a tour of the George Eastman house."

"Okay, but you must tell me who that is first."

"He was the founder of Eastman Kodak company."

"As in the film?"

"Yes, ma'am."

"Interesting. Let's do it."

Lincoln pays my tab, even though I said I could pay for myself and then we head out. We catch a cab outside the hotel. I am kinda curious, why he chose to go to this house. I haven't dated anyone who's ever asked me if I wanted to go to such a place before. I think it is cool and different. If this is any indication of how our month will go, it will be refreshing.

As we travel through the small city, traffic is nothing like New York City where I live.

Out of the corner of my eye, I peek over to him. Lincoln seems to be the kind of man that is tender, kind, and caring. It didn't go unnoticed today how much he was in tune with me. By that I mean he pays attention and listens. I have dated a few men in the past that would cut me off whenever I spoke. As if my opinion didn't matter at all. It was as if I didn't have a mind of my own. It was basically their way of thinking no matter the situation. They sometimes even told me how I should be feeling. I keep getting snippets of how I've been with the wrong guys my entire life. How could I have gotten everything so wrong up until now? Can I even trust my own judgment to pick the right guy now? What if I get it wrong and choose a man who isn't right for me?

"What are you thinking about?"

"That I've dated the wrong people in the past. I don't know if I can trust myself to pick who is right for me. A December wedding seems reckless."

"How did you figure out you've dated the wrong people?"

"Going through this experience Grams set up."

"Once a person sees what a relationship was lacking and they learn what it is to be with someone as an equal, they don't tend to settle anymore. I don't believe you will make the wrong choice. I've been dealing with couples for years. I have seen a train wreck waiting to happen and I have witnessed true love. From the short amount of time we've been together, I think you'll end up in the true love category."

"Thank you. I needed to hear that."

Going to the George Eastman house I learned that the reason Lincoln brought me there was because it's just another example of what he does. He said capturing every moment of the day that you dream about, you have to have the right exposure, the right couple, and the right atmosphere. For your memories to be captured to its full extent, you need the right person behind the lens. Lincoln really cares about his career and making people happy. He is a very humble person. I don't know much about him, but I like what I see already.

Once we left the mansion, we headed out to dinner at a fancy restaurant. Upon arriving, I see grams talking to a man I do not know. By the looks of the way he's looking at her, I'd say Grams has an admirer. I think it's sweet of Lincoln to ask Gram's friend Gary to join us.

I couldn't help but notice some of the looks we received as we were walking to our table. It's hard to believe that people still can't wrap their heads around a white woman being courted by a beautiful, handsome, black man. I'm not going to let the looks of disgust ruin what could be a beautiful relationship forming. I was half tempted to grab Lincoln and kiss him right there to show people friendships have no color. Neither does love. The heart wants what the heart wants, that's what people should see.

CHAPTER EIGHT
LINCOLN

I have met a lot of people in my lifetime and I have to admit Ciara is a genuine person. I am enjoying her company immensely so far. I like the way she smiles. I like the way she slaps my upper arm when I crack a joke and make her laugh. Mostly, I like her personality. She is real, she doesn't portray herself as someone she is not. I've met many fake people being surrounded by celebrities, Ciara is far from being fake.

Ciara seemed to really enjoy the place I took her to today. I liked sharing with her why I took her there. Photography is a big deal when you want your memories to reflect one of the most important days of your life. I am hopeful dinner will be just as impressive. Tracy sent me a list of restaurants earlier, the one I chose is a fine dining experience for this evening.

After all, I have two very fine ladies to impress this evening.

"Are you from here?"

"I grew up in the area, but I don't live here anymore. I reside in Hollywood now."

"How long have you lived there?"

"The last seven years. Once my business took off, I moved out there since I do a lot of weddings for celebrities."

"Who was your first?"

"I cannot disclose that information. I signed a nondisclosure agreement. But that wedding put me in the spotlight. I had so many phone calls afterward."

"That's really cool, even if you can't talk about it."

"How about you? How long have you been designing clothing?"

"Just about all my life. I love it. It helps that Grams taught me everything she knows."

"That is pretty cool that you followed in her footsteps."

"A lot of people I have met said I ride her coattails."

"I find that to be absurd. You two have very much different styles."

"We do, but it's more like I use the MV clothing line instead of breaking out my own line."

"Don't let people determine who you are or how you got there. Many families carry on the family business."

"And your family, what do they do?"

"My father worked for Kodak and took early retirement. My mother was a stay-at-home mother."

"Nice."

We arrive at the restaurant and I see Millie waiting outside for us. She is also striking up a conversation with someone. Millie has always been a social butterfly ever since I met her about five years ago. We got to know each other at a wedding I was doing. Millie had people on the dance floor, dancing all night long. Including me. She definitely brings the fun. To me, it's hard to believe she never married. Maybe she realizes what she has missed out on and that is why she did all this for Ciara.

When we approach Millie, she introduces us to a man around her age. We learn, or I should say, I learn Millie and he are old friends who just happened to bump into one another. I did the polite thing and invited him to join us for dinner. I might have a slight agenda by doing this, after all, nobody really wants to feel like the third wheel.

CHAPTER 8

The four of us enter Mannings as the hostess leads us to our table, I already am wishing I chose a different dining experience. I see the looks I am getting. A black man holding a white woman's hand isn't very welcoming. Ciara notices the looks as well. Once we are seated, Gary, the gentleman occupying Millie, doesn't sit at the table. The hostess gives him a quizzical glance before handing out the menus to the rest of us. I hope he isn't going to make a scene. It will cause me to look worse than I already do. I have thick skin. I can handle a few ignorant looks.

Gary leans over the table and in a low voice he says, *"I am uncomfortable surrounding myself with assholes."*

"I hear that," Millie replies and Ciara nods her head.

I smile, knowing I am in good company with some amazing people. *"Where shall we go?"*

'Anywhere but here is fine with me," Ciara says.

"I had dinner at a lovely place last night. It isn't far from here."

Millie stands from the table and says, *"Let's go."*

Ciara joins Millie in standing, so I do as well. I have no problem with getting the hell out of here. Ciara takes my hand as we walk back through the dining room. She stops dead smack in the middle. I am as shocked as the other guest when she kisses me. Holy hell, was it hot! She can kiss me a thousand more times like that and it still might not be enough. I have to remember why I am part of Ciara's journey. Though it's not going to be easy if she kisses me like that again.

Ciara and I follow behind Gary and Millie. He didn't say where we were going, so I must keep my eye on him. Traffic isn't too bad, but I don't want to be blamed for losing them. I am not gonna lie, my mind is still on that kiss. I want to know if she did it to piss people off. Actually, I want to know if she felt the same spark as I did. I would love to know what is going on inside her head.

We ended up having a low key dinner at NickTahou's. By low key I mean we had the famous garbage plate. I have had many of them in my lifetime and love them. I have missed having them since moving to Hollywood. It thrilled me to know Ciara never had one before and loved it. You can't visit this city without trying it once.

Millie left with Gary after we chowed down our meals. I think Gary is smitten with Millie, maybe

CHAPTER 8

harboring some old feelings. He has that look in his eyes I see all the time, from guys in love. I am not so sure Millie reciprocates those feelings. She seems to enjoy his company, but I am not so sure love is on her agenda. Now Ciara is a bit harder to read. I cannot tell if she likes me or if that kiss was just to make a point to small-minded people. We just met, so I am leaning toward making a point, which I adore. Ciara's actions tell me she has no problem with my skin color.

"So, Mr. Titus, what are we going to do now that our stomachs are full?"

"As much as I would love to take you out on the town and show you off, I actually have work tomorrow."

"You do? Another bridal show?"

"Even better, a wedding. I am trying to figure out who the lucky guy is, the groom, or me. The groom is marrying the love of his life, but I get to have this gorgeous girl on my arm tomorrow, so it's pretty much a tossup."

"Oh, I get to go with you? Whose wedding is it?"

"My sister's. I would love for you to be by my side tomorrow."

"Wow, that is awesome. I can't wait."

"Are you excited to see me in action?"

"I am, but even more excited I get to be your date. I love weddings."

"Have you checked out the grounds at your hotel?"

"I had breakfast outdoors on the patio this morning."

"How about I take you back to the hotel and show you around?"

"I'd like that."

I purposely booked Ciara's suite at The Woodcliff. That is where my sister will marry tomorrow. The place is beautiful. She couldn't have picked a better location. Truthfully, I picked it and she agreed to it without hesitation.

CHAPTER NINE
CIARA

Spending time with Lincoln all day yesterday is a day I won't soon forget. Besides him being a wonderful man, I learned a great deal from being with him. I am not talking about his bridal show or the Eastman house. I am talking about what happened at the restaurant. It angered me. Last night was an eye-opener to something I didn't know was a problem. How can people be so judgmental? They don't know us. All they saw was skin color and that's not okay with me. I didn't feel angry for myself, I felt angry for Lincoln at all those asshats. He's such a good-hearted person that he was willing to sit in a restaurant full of haters just to impress me and Grams. I was so elated that Gary spoke up. I wanted to drag Lincoln out of that shithole. Those people didn't deserve the privilege to be in the same room as him. Once we got the hell out of there, our evening was fantastic. The food was outstanding at the next place we went to. A little odd at first as it looks like a hot mess, but I got a taste of the hot sauce and I was done for. I have to say the best part of the evening was the walk around the hotel. I saw just how beautiful the place was at night. I'm looking forward to seeing how the wedding area looks in the daytime. Lincoln told me once the sun starts to set, the view is incredible. I am hoping to catch the sunset tonight if I am able to sneak away.

 Lincoln walked me to my suite last night and said goodnight. We didn't share another kiss. Part of me wanted him to kiss me and another part of me was happy with it being a simple goodnight. I like him, but I don't want to jump into anything too quickly. When I kissed him at the restaurant, it was sort of wrong for me to do. I don't fully regret it because I was making a point. I do, however, feel I pushed past a line I wasn't ready to cross, yet. I'm not prepared for falling in love with another man. I have enough emotions to sort out as it is. Porter is right, at some point I do have to figure out where my heart truly lies. That doesn't mean it has to be today.

 I already took a shower and got dressed in casual clothing. I've been thinking about going to breakfast on the patio again. Lincoln told me he has golf this morning with the wedding partying and won't be free until late morning. I have about four hours to kill. If I don't grab something to eat now, I will be waiting a while since the reception isn't until this early evening. I could see if Grams was still around and ask her to join me. It would be nice to have her company. It's hard to catch up with one another with others around.

Just as I was about to call grams there was a knock on my door. At first, I thought Grams might've had the same idea as me, but once I opened the door there was a young lady that I did not know. She introduced herself as Lincoln's sister. I invited her in and we sat and talked for about a half-hour, getting to know one another. Bella is super sweet. She doesn't seem nervous at all about getting married today at all. Eventually, she told me that she had to go have breakfast with her wedding party and that she came to invite me to join them. I happily accepted. I met with all the girls that are in the wedding, and they are all as sweet as she is. I didn't feel like an outsider at all which is very nice. Breakfast was a wonderful display buffet style. I like that since everyone likes different foods. It was nice that the hot foods were actually still hot and not dried out or overdone. It really was perfect.

Once breakfast was over and we had killed over an hour, they all had to go get their hair and nails done, so we wrapped it up. Bella invited me to join them for that as well. I didn't want to overstay my welcome and was a little hesitant to go, but she said that she would love to have me, so I accepted that invitation as well. I am getting my first glance of what my wedding day could be like, except I don't have as many friends as Bella does.

Lincoln ended up coming to find me just when I was all done getting my hair done. I thanked the girls for including me before I went off with him. I thought that we were heading to my suite but I came to find out, there is a door in my suite that connects to his room. I saw the door and knew it connected to another room, I just didn't think the room adjoining was his.

Lincoln wanted to change out of his golfing attire and put on some shorts. I saw his tuxedo hanging. It didn't occur to me that he might actually be in the wedding. It makes sense now that I think about it.

CHAPTER 9

Once he changed into something cooler to wear, he asked me to accompany him while he checked on the wedding preparation. Even though he's in the wedding he is still the coordinator. Of course, I accepted.

As we were heading outdoors, I was joking around with him when I said, *"I'm starting to think I'm dating you to see what all to expect for my future wedding."* His reaction was telling. I think I hit the nail on the head.

"Our entire month won't all be about planning and attending weddings. June was too booked for me to take a lot of time off."

I decide to play it cool. *"So, this isn't the only wedding we will be attending?"*

"Nope. I have one in two weeks in California. I do have plans for tomorrow that I think you will enjoy."

I am tempted to ask if he had to bid on me at all. I decided today isn't the day to get into that sort of conversation. I'm just going to relax and enjoy the day with him. I do enjoy his company. Lincoln is such a laid back kind of guy. He seems to keep his cool even under stress. I saw that first hand when something wasn't the way it was supposed to be with the outdoor seating. He told the workers what was wrong very nicely then moved on. He talks to people as he would want to be talked to. I respect that immensely. I hate when someone has power and they talk down to hourly employees. The more I am around Lincoln, the more I am enjoying getting to know him.

CHAPTER TEN
LINCOLN

When I was out golfing with the boys today Ciara was consuming my mind. I barely know the girl, but I can't seem to get her off my mind. I'm starting to not care about the deal that I have with Millie. I want a real chance of getting this woman with no strings attached. I know that I am like the sixth guy, but I think I still might have a chance of capturing her heart. I am a true romantic at heart, so if there's a chance I think I'm gonna grab it. I know that you have to expect the unexpected when it comes to love. So why not me? Why can't it be my time to be the groom instead of just the coordinator? I think Ciara is liking me, so why not see where this month could lead? Even though I think she caught on to the purpose of me dating her, I could still have a chance. Time is such an unpredictable thing.

Ciara is with me now and I can't stop taking

glances at her. She really gets my heart pitter-pattering. I'm supposed to be chillin' with the guys after I checked that everything is running smoothly, but I'd rather be with her. She is definitely better to look at.

"It was really nice of your sister to include me this morning. I have a feeling you were behind that, so thank you."

"You are welcome. I figured it would be a nice way to get to know her."

"Will I be meeting your parents?"

"You will." I check the time on my watch. *"They should actually be arriving within the next half-hour."*

"Great! I'm looking forward to meeting them."

"Since I'm in the wedding, I have you seated with your grandmother."

"I was wondering if she was still here."

"My mother and Millie are quite tight. I introduced them a few years back and they keep in touch often. Millie is my mother's go-to designer whenever she needs a new outfit."

"That's great. Sometimes I think Grams knows the entire world."

"I could use a drink, care to join me for a cocktail?"

"I'd love to."

CHAPTER 10

I hold out my hand and she takes it. Today might be a tossup with who'll be more happy, my sister, or me. Naturally, I want my sister to be the happiest. After all, she's only getting married once.

We find a cozy spot at the bar indoors. It's getting to a point that it's pretty warm outside. I prefer to stay cool until the wedding. Soon enough, all the guys will want out of their tuxedos. I am so glad that my sister took my advice and went with air conditioning in the tent. Otherwise, we'd all be a heaping mess covered in sweat.

"Would you like something to eat, maybe an appetizer or something light? Dinner isn't for another three hours."

"I'm good. I kinda over-ate at breakfast."

"What can I get you to drink?"

"How about a Whipped vodka and orange juice."

"You got it!"

When the bartender comes our way, I order our drinks. It doesn't take her long at all to make Ciara's drink and pour my locally made draft beer.

"Thank you for the drink."

"You are welcome."

"What is on the menu for dinner?"

"Bella went with buffet style. So there is a

chicken, primed rib, or fish choice with five different side dishes."

"Do most people go with a buffet style?"

"It's about 50/50. The people who prefer to sit-down, believe it's more classy. I like buffet style because it's easier."

"Seems sit-down is more of a headache because you have to get orders ahead of time, correct?" I nod my head. *"I noticed when looking at invitations that some had extra cards for meal choices."*

I really want to change the subject. I know I'm supposed to be encouraging wedding stuff, but I would rather get to know her instead.

"See why it takes time to plan?"

She lets out a sigh. *"I do."*

"Tell me something I don't know about you."

"Hmm."

"Whatever pops into your head first."

"I was dead set against Grams silent auction when I found out about it."

"And now? Are you still against it?"

"Not really. I've been learning more about myself. I think I'm becoming a stronger person. I dated many jerks, I've learned."

"Nothing wrong with growth."

"Okay, your turn."

"I was a professional baseball player for two years, but I quit playing before my third year."

"Really, how come?"

"In college, a friend of mine was getting married and she didn't have a clue what to do. I helped her out and I truly enjoyed it, so I quit baseball to pursue my career of being a wedding planner."

She giggles and slaps my upper arm. *"Well that's good, I already dated a baseball player."*

"I know. I actually played with Warrick. We were both rookies the same year."

"Small world, I guess."

I check my phone when it goes off. My parents have arrived. We take our drinks with us and then go to greet them in the lobby. I cross my fingers that they are impressed with Ciara as much as I am. Their approval means a great deal to me.

Soon after my parents arrived it was time for me to get ready. I walked Ciara back to her suite and grabbed my tuxedo before I left to get ready with the guys. I didn't want to leave her alone to fend for herself. She assured me she'd be fine on her own, besides she wasn't entirely going to be alone with

Millie attending the wedding. For the next hour and a half, she was on my mind. I was excited to be with her again. I pictured her in my mind all dressed up in formal wear. When I saw her as I passed by, walking down the aisle, what I pictured wasn't even close to how beautiful she looked. I am one hell of a lucky guy to be dating her for the rest of the month. I know if she finds out I'm a business deal, it may destroy my chance with her. I have thought about telling her. Maybe I should step up and just tell Millie I cannot follow through on my end. Losing the business of being Ciara's wedding planner is one worth losing out on, especially if I get the girl in the end.

I was extremely honored to have Ciara by my side during the hour it took for photos. She could have gone off with the rest of the guests to enjoy cocktails and appetizers, but she chose to stay by my side.

Once we get through dinner, I won't have to be separated from Ciara for the rest of the evening. I am looking forward to having a dance or two with her in my arms. I feel like a little boy with a huge crush. I haven't had such an attraction to a woman as this since my last real relationship back in college. Hell, this attraction feels strong. I thought back then that Cassie was the woman I'd someday marry. We were in a relationship for three years before we both realized we wanted different things in life. I think she was more interested in the money I'd make being a professional ballplayer than being in love with me. In the short time I've known Ciara, I can tell she could care less about money and someone's popularity status. She isn't about that at all. Seeing many relationships in my line of work, you learn to read people's body language, attitudes, and personality. It's an advantage I'll use to someday find the right person for me. I haven't had a long-lasting relationship since Cassie because I can see a train wreck waiting to happen. This is why I feel I need to be honest with Ciara what my purpose is for dating her this month. Honesty can go a long way. Real relationships can happen when least expected.

CHAPTER ELEVEN
CIARA

The wedding was such a gorgeous ceremony. Bella is a stunning bride. You can literally see the glow of happiness radiating off of her. The love the two of them have for one another seeps from their pores. I hope when my wedding day comes it is as evident the love we share with one another is as true as theirs. I can't help but wish I could be a person standing outside the relationships I've had with Malcolm, Hawk, Warrick, Kaiden, and Gaetano to see if I have that glow Bella has for her new husband, Martin. I know that isn't possible. I have to find a way to figure out my feelings for each one of them. Attending this wedding today, I realize it's not going to be easy. I have real feelings for each one of the guys I've been with. Now, I'm just adding more feelings to the mix by being with Lincoln. I genuinely am liking him. I was hoping I wouldn't. I was hopeful to make this already difficult choice easier on myself by not having a connection with him.

I snuck away from the wedding reception. Honestly, I am a little overwhelmed. I have this gut feeling Grams purposely put Lincoln this month. First the bridal show and now this wedding. Learning there will be another one we will be attending later this month seems all too much of coincidence. I am trying to figure out if Lincoln is supposed to be a man I am dating or if he's really meant to be a pawn. I want to ask, but I'm risking wrecking what could be a beautiful relationship if I am wrong. I wish my mind would just shut off and I would enjoy the happy moment I should be having.

I ventured out to where Lincoln told me the sunset is beautiful to see. I have a seat on the bench and watch as the sun slowly settles. He was right, it's breathtaking the way it seems it falls off the cliff. It's very peaceful out here and I could sit here for hours if I weren't supposed to be having a good time elsewhere.

"May I join you?"

I tilt my head to see Lincoln standing off to the side of the bench. He took off his bow tie and tuxedo jacket. His shirt is unbuttoned to his chest area.

"Yes, you may."

He sits next to me, putting his arm around my shoulders. I scoot closer to him and rest my head on his shoulder. We haven't said anything for quite some time. Eventually, I break the silence.

"It's as beautiful as you said it would be."

"It is. There's only one thing that is more beautiful at this moment."

"Oh ya? What is that?"

"You."

I lift my head and look him in the eye. Maybe I am wrong and he's not a pawn. Why does this entire journey have to be so damn difficult?

"I want to kiss you," he says in a soft voice.

It's almost as if he is unsure if I want him to kiss me. I don't say a word because I'm unsure of where this is going. He leans in closer. I am not going to stop him. I want to know if this is real. Once his lips meet mine, it's soft and tender. I feel myself relax and let the kiss happen naturally. Lincoln is a good kisser. I'll give him that much.

We stayed out on the cliff long enough to see the sunset. I told him we better head back to the reception. He agreed. When we got back, it was time for the cake. It was sweet to see them lovingly feed each other a piece. I was happy Lincoln and I didn't miss it. Next came the first dance, then the rest of the evening was lots of dancing and a few cocktails. The wedding couldn't have been more perfect.

Lincoln had a few things to attend to so I decided to call it a night. I came back to my suite to get out of my dress, then took my hair down. I jumped into the shower to wash the days sweat away. I was just about to crawl into bed when I heard my phone notify me of a text message. I smiled when I saw it was Lincoln. He asked me to come to my door. I hurried and put on a pair of night shorts and a top. I opened the door to this gorgeous man and he cupped my face and kissed me.

"I couldn't go to bed without giving you a good night kiss."

I leaned on the doorframe and watched him go to his door. A part of me wanted to invite him in. Another part of me was relieved he went to his own room. This just keeps getting more and more complicated. More feelings are joining the heaping pile I already have built up for the other guys. This is becoming completely unfair. How am I ever going to be as happy as Bella with so many wonderful men to choose from? A December wedding is looking as if it's not going to happen. I'm going to need a decade to figure out my emotions.

I fell right to sleep last night. I wasn't aware I was that tired. Once I fell into a deep sleep, I woke from a dream I was having. In my dream, I was in the wedding gown my grandma made for me in my old bedroom. It was my wedding day. I peeked out the window to see the garden covered in light snow. It was pretty with all the lights turned on. I turned my attention to the door expecting to see Grams or Porter. Instead, it was my groom sneaking in to see me. I don't know who it was. I woke before I said his name. Now that I am awake, I don't know whose face it was that I saw. I heard once, a long time ago if you dream of your wedding day and you see the face of the man, it's who you will really marry. My dream hadn't helped me at all with my current situation if that myth is true. I'm still in the dark with my own wedding.

When I crawl out of bed. I'm left with the feeling that my life is going in the right direction. Whoever it was in my dream, I was filled with love for him. I am going to have a happy ever after, eventually. Just knowing that puts a smile on my face. I just have to make it a few more months and a couple more guys until I say I do to the person I can't live without.

I go down the spiral stairs to answer the knock on

the door. I am assuming it's Lincoln. I put a smile on my face before I open the door. I am stunned when it isn't him at all. After I took my jaw off the floor, I pulled him into my room and then peered out into the hallway to see if anyone saw anything. As soon as I shut the door I am spun around, my back is pushed against it. I moaned into his mouth when he dominantly kissed me.

CHAPTER TWELVE
LINCOLN

Yesterday was simply wonderful. My sister's wedding couldn't have run any smoother if it tried. I was thrilled with the outcome. She made a beautiful bride and all of her dreams were fulfilled. Having Ciara as my date made it all the better. I cannot imagine sharing this precious moment with any other woman.

After I entered my room last night, I was wishing Ciara invited me into her suite. Having her curled up next to me in bed would have been the perfect ending to the day. I am not trying to rush anything. I want this relationship to flow on its own naturally. If this relationship is going to happen, I want it built on solid ground. If she would have invited me in, of course, I would have accepted. I wouldn't have turned down the opportunity to spend more time with her.

Today is a new day. I have every intention of

spending as much time with her as I can. I already made plans for our day together, starting with room service. After that, we'll be leaving The Woodcliff and heading west. Tonight will be our last night in upstate New York. Come tomorrow afternoon we will be on a plane heading to my home in Hollywood. I have a little work to do, but most of my time is free to be with her. I am going to do my damnedest to win her over. By the end of our month together, I hope I make a good enough of an impression on her that I beat out all the other guys. I could really see being a life long partner to Ciara.

I already called down for breakfast to be delivered to my room. I rub my hands together when the knock comes on my door. It's time to surprise Ciara with breakfast.

I wheel the cart into my room and over to the door that adjoins our rooms. I knock on it and wait. I am hopeful that she hasn't been up long enough to already order something. It's only seven, there is the possibility that she's not even awake yet. If she's a heavy sleeper, she might not even hear my knock. As the seconds pass, maybe I should call her room. Just when I step away, I hear the locks clicking. I smile when the door opens.

"Good morning!"

"Morning," she says.

Is it just me or does she look a little flushed? She seems a little out of breath, as well.

"I took the liberty of ordering you breakfast."

"Oh… Umm… you really didn't need to do that, but thank you."

She's definitely acting a little rattled. *"Did I wake you?"*

"You did, but it's fine."

I look at the spiral staircase and back to her. *"I can just leave the breakfast with you."*

She finger combs her hair. *"You know, I was having the strangest dream. I am glad you woke me. No need for me to eat alone when I have such a kind man delivering me food."*

She opens the door wider allowing me in. I push the cart through the door and leave it next to the dining table. She lifts a lid off one of the plates and smiles.

"I love bagels and the coffee smells wonderful."

We set up the table, then I watch as she pours the coffee into the mugs for us. She takes a bagel then adds cream cheese and strawberry jam. She moans as she takes a bite. I've noticed she does that when she really likes something. I remember during the bridal show she did it for the first time with the white cake with raspberry filling between the layers.

"You have a little something right here."

I use my thumb to wipe cream cheese from the corner of her mouth. Man, do I want to lean in closer and kiss her. Every bit of my body wants to touch her, feel her skin upon mine. My fingers are dying to feel her erect nipples beneath them. I move my eyes off her chest and back to my plate. My manhood is growing hard in my jogging pants. If I want to stand from this table without an erection, I need to stop with the sexual thoughts. Lord, she makes that nearly impossible, though. Ever since I laid my eyes on her I have wanted to touch every inch of her body. I seriously need to stop thinking!

"We will be leaving as soon as you are ready."

"Where are we going?"

"Tomorrow we will be heading to my home in California, but before we do that I want to take you somewhere else."

"Are you going to give me a hint?"

"We'll be outdoors most of the day."

She laughs. *"That isn't much of a hint. How am I supposed to pick the right outfit to wear?"*

I checked the weather app on my phone. *"Looks*

like it's a hot one, so shorts and a tank top should work."

"So dress casual, got it."

We finish eating and as much as I don't want to leave, I know the sooner I do, the sooner she is packed and ready to go. That means she's mine for the rest of the day and evening. So, I stand from the table and wheel the cart out into the hallway. I asked her approximately how much time she needed and she said about an hour. I left to pack my own things in my room. I hated hearing her locking the door between us.

Since I didn't unpack my suitcase fully, I don't have that much to do. Grabbing all my belongings only takes a few minutes, so I decided to go see if my parents are still around after I take my luggage to the rental car. I'm not sure when the next time will be when I'll see them again. I won't mind catching my sister before she takes off for her honeymoon as well.

I saw my parents entering the outdoor patio area when returning from the car. So, I head in that direction. I sat and talked with them for quite some time while they had a bite to eat. We talked about the wedding and how well everything ran. Talk turned to Ciara. My mother being a mother, she asked about how serious we are. I broke down and told her the

CHAPTER 12

deal I have with Millie. I also told her how I didn't expect to like her as much as I do. Both of my parents have concerns and both agreed I must be truthful with Ciara as to why she's really with me this month. Starting a relationship with a white lie isn't the best way to build trust. I agree with them for the most part. Once they ate, they were ready to go home. Neither one of them is too comfortable in places that aren't home. I decided to walk them out to their car. I give my father a hug then my mother.

As I enter the hotel I run into Millie.

"Good morning, Millie."

"Good morning, Lincoln. What a lovely wedding. I'm looking forward to seeing how Ciara's wedding is planned."

"About that..."

She cuts me. *"Second-guessing our deal?"*

"I'm not sure. I really like Ciara."

"You cannot back out of our deal. I need to see my granddaughter married by the end of the year."

"One thing I haven't been able to figure out, why are you pushing for her to marry so hard?"

Millie looks away from me. She watches a man walk through the lobby and her lips curled up to a smile. When she puts her attention back on me, she says, *"I have my reasons that I'm not willing to discuss today. Stick to our deal."* She takes a few steps away and turns back toward me. *"I never said you couldn't fall in love with each other. Your time is short, I suggest you use your time wisely, Mr. Titus because she's already in love with more than one man."*

With that, I am left with more uncertainty. Do I tell Ciara about my arrangement with her grandmother or keep that a secret? The bigger question is, do I risk getting my heart crushed from a woman already in love with other men?

CHAPTER THIRTEEN
CIARA

That was the most uncomfortable breakfast in the history of my life. I had to sit there and pretend I didn't have a man hiding upstairs. When the knock came between our two rooms, I didn't know what to do, so I sent my surprise visitor into hiding. As soon as Lincoln left, I locked the door and felt a bit of relief. I also felt bad that Lincoln had no idea I was hiding a secret. I'm supposed to be dating him, not hiding one of the other guys I have already been with.

I run up the stairs as fast as I can. My jaw hits the floor once again. I put my hands on my hips to show I'm not pleased with the situation he put me in.

"Kaiden Marcellus, why did you do that to me? You know we aren't supposed to be doing this. What on earth are you doing here?"

"Come here," he says, patting the bed next to him.

My eyes go to his bare upper body. *"No, explain to me first."*

"I had to see you. I can't stop thinking about you and I miss you more than I've ever missed anyone."

My hands fall from my hips. My body is screaming for me to go to him. My brain isn't far behind my body's thinking.

"Kaiden…"

"Ciara, come here."

It takes all of my willpower to shake my head no. Kaiden gets off the bed and comes to stand in front of me. He lifts a hand to the back of my head and grabs a fist full of my hair. He then tugs my head backward and kisses me. I feel myself melting into a heaping pile of lust and desire. I give in and grab him, bringing his body closer to my own. This man drives my body crazy. My heart thumps in my chest. My feelings for him run deep within me. I cannot control how badly I want him.

Kaiden lifts my night tank top up and over my breasts. I moan when his palms run over my perky nipples. I should put a stop to this, but I don't fucking want to.

"Did I hear you need a shower?"

CHAPTER 13

I nod my head yes then my nightshirt is taken completely off. I moan when his hands slip into the waistband of my night shorts. They soon fall to the floor, pooling around my feet. He steps back and his eyes travel over my body. He then steps around me and spanks my butt.

"*Hey!*"

"*Shower, Ciara.*"

I spin on my heels and watch Kaiden turn on the water. I walk the few feet there is and stand just outside the shower.

"*Time is of the essence.*"

I peek down at his jeans. It's one thing having shower sex over FaceTime, it's another to have him here in the flesh, so I reach out for the button of his jeans and unbutton them. When I get them open, his cock is hard and springs free. I get into the shower, leaving his jeans still on.

"*Time is of the essence, Mr. Marcellus.*"

I tilt my head back, letting the water cascade over my dark locks. Closing my eyes when his hand comes to my pussy. I spread my legs further apart, letting him have full access to my body.

"*Such a naughty girl allowing me to break the rules.*"

. *"I don't care...,"* Kaiden's fingers enter me, *"about the rules."*

"Christ, I miss your moans and how wet you get for me."

His mouth sucks a nipple between his lips. His teeth graze the erect nipple and my nails comb through his hair. I fist his hair as his thumb finds my clit and teeth sink into my skin.

"Kaiden, I..."

My words are lost when he lifts me off my feet and I wrap my wet legs around his drenched body. My back hits the shower tile. My arms tightly grip onto his neck as he enters my pussy. I love having him inside me, using my body for his pleasure.

It does not take long for my orgasm to come. Every single part of me feels the effects he has on me.

"I love you, Ciara. I wanted to wait to tell you those words until I knew if we'd be together, but I couldn't wait any longer for you to know. I don't know how I am going to survive if you are not in my life."

I gaze into his eyes. He's telling me the truth. I have the power to ruin his life if we don't end up together. I don't want to be that person. I know my feelings are real for him. I also know I have real feelings for other men as well.

"I love you, too, Kaiden."

"I don't want to leave. I want to kidnap you and begin our life together right this second."

I don't know what to say to that. My heart is screaming for him to do just that and melting at the same time. My head is telling me I still have to sort out my other feelings. Him showing up like this makes things more complicated than they already were.

"I wish I could allow that to happen."

"You better finish getting washed up."

He steps out of the shower. He doesn't even dry off before slipping his jeans on. I get out. There's no way he's sneaking out. Not like this anyway.

"Kaiden," I say, grabbing his arm, *"don't you dare think you're leaving while I'm in the shower."*

"I don't know what to do. I want you in my life. I'm not sleeping. I barely eat. I think about you every second of the day. No matter what I do, you consume my mind. I've never been a jealous man, but I cannot stand knowing you are with other men. It's driving me absolutely crazy thinking you slept with my brother. I hate not knowing if I am your future."

Tears are filling my eyes quicker than I can wipe them away. *"I didn't sleep with him. I haven't had sex with anyone since you. I want to tell you this is over, but that wouldn't be me being honest with you. I don't want you to think we are going to be together after this over because it may not be true. I also want to tell you to wait for me. I am confused. I do love you, Kaiden. I know that for sure. However, I also fell in love with other guys."*

Kaiden sits on the foot of the bed. He grabs my hand and pulls me to him. His arms tangle around my waist in a hug. His cheek rests on my chest. I run my finger through his hair.

"I'm sorry. I shouldn't have put this on you. I am a strong man in most things. You, Ciara, are my weakness. As much as I hate this entire situation, I'll be alright. I don't want you to worry about me, okay?"

"I do worry, though. I worry every day that passes that the one I love won't be there at the end. I worry that I'm going to hurt people that I don't want to hurt. I fear that I will go through all of this and I end up alone. I am risking every relationship that I have had."

"I came here to tell you how much I am in love with you. I couldn't wait another day to tell you."

"I am glad you did. I already knew, but it feels really good hearing it."

"I better get out of here before Lincoln sends out

a search party for you."

The tears I've been crying come on stronger. I don't want to let him go. I feel like I can't breathe. It breaks my heart knowing I may hurt one of the best men I've ever known.

Kaiden stands from the bed and gets his shirt and puts it on. I turn my back to him. My voice cracks when I ask, *"If I didn't love you as much as I do, I probably would have slept with your brother. I couldn't do that to you or tarnish what we have."*

His arms come around me. His lips are near my neck. *"Thank you, I really needed to hear that."* He kisses my cheek. *"I'll be here whenever you are ready to start a life with me. I'll always be here no matter what happens."*

I lose his warmth when he moves away from me. I close my eyes as I hear his footsteps going down the stairs. I keep my feet planted so that I don't chase after him. Once I hear the door close, I start tossing my clothes into a suitcase frantically. I keep wiping my cheeks as the tears keep flowing. I go into the bathroom and see that the shower is still on. What am I doing? I feel all sorts of messed up. How the hell am I going to be able to spend the day with Lincoln after what happened with Kaiden? I don't think I can do it. I search for my phone. I need to talk to someone.

CHAPTER FOURTEEN
LINCOLN

I went to see if Ciara was ready to leave and she didn't answer her door. I assumed she might have been in the shower or something. I sent her a text telling her I'd be waiting for her in the lobby. I already turned in the key to my room and didn't feel like going back out on the patio. When I didn't get a reply, I headed back to the lobby where I found a cozy spot on a love seat.

Another forty-five minutes pass before I see her step off the elevator. Right away I could see something different about her. I get up and go to help her with her luggage. It is then that I see her eyes are a bit puffy and red. My instincts are telling me to give her a hug and ask if she's alright. I wonder what could have possibly happened in the time I left her to pack to now. Anything could have happened in the two hours time span. We got out to the car and I put her belongings in the trunk with mine. She got in the car while I went back inside the hotel to check her out. It's not until I am driving away that she speaks to me.

"Can we stop at a gas station or store so that I can buy a pair of sunglasses?"

"Absolutely. I am not sure what time the mall opens, but I can check and see if they are open."

"A gas station is fine if they're not open. I don't want to slow down your plans."

"It isn't far from here. We don't really have a time table today."

"Okay, thanks."

The mall wasn't open, so I stopped at a gas station for her. Ciara goes back to being quiet. I still want to ask her what's the matter, but I can sense she's not ready to talk. It bothers me to see her upset. I want to hold her and tell her whatever it is that is bothering her, it will get better.

Twenty minutes into our drive I turn the radio's volume up higher and start singing Night Moves. She burst out laughing at my poor attempt to sing a little Bob. I am glad to hear her laughing, even if it is at my expense.

"I think you missed your calling. You should have

been a professional singer." She tries to hide more laughter, but I can't.

"There's always time to start a new adventure."

I pull into the zoo another fifteen minutes or so later. Her smile got really big. She tells me she loves the zoo, but no way in hell is she going in the snake building. I tease her a little bit about how I'm going to drag her inside. Little does she know, I skip that part as well.

After we spent hours at the zoo we headed to our next destination. We talked about the best part and we both agreed it was having ice cream cones while watching the seals swim and do tricks with the zookeeper. The day really changed Ciara's mood. I'm glad that I could be the one to lift her spirits.

We traveled to Niagara Falls. We walked for miles enjoying each other's company and the falls. Ciara has never been here before, so we did all the must-dos while being here. Nothing says Niagara Falls as going on the Maid of the Mist does.

I already made dinner reservations at a nice

CHAPTER 14

restaurant when I planned this trip, however, we spent so much time enjoying the falls that we missed it. We ended up having dinner and drinks at the Hard Rock Cafe.

During dinner, we overheard a couple talking about the fireworks that are happening tonight. I didn't even have to ask if she'd like to see them, the smile was a dead giveaway that she did. Once we left the restaurant we walked back to the falls to find a place to sit.

"I've only been here once this time of year. My father always brought us in the winter for the Festival of Lights. I swear it was always the coldest day of the year."

"Thank you for bringing me here and the zoo. I've loved them both."

"My father took us to the Buffalo zoo then here. My sister and I slept the whole way home. We were so cold that we snuggled under a blanket together."

"Aww, you shared a family tradition with me! I feel honored, Lincoln."

"It's been my pleasure." She leans her head on my shoulder. *"I could tell something changed with you this morning. I'm glad to see your smile again."*

She doesn't say anything. I take that as she

doesn't want to talk about it. I'm not going to push the issue, but I wish she'd open up to me.

We stay for the entire fireworks show. We actually moved from our spot to get a better view of them reflecting off the falls. It was absolutely beautiful to see. I am blessed enough to experience this with her. As much as I'd like to spend another day or two here, we have a flight to catch in the morning. We found a hotel with openings and got a room. I didn't make reservations in advance because I was unsure if it would be for one room or two. Due to not booking a room, we had to share a room. Ciara didn't seem to mind. I certainly didn't mind at all.

She changed into nightclothes and crawled into bed. When I put on some gym shorts, I joined her. She curled up next to me and said goodnight. Having her body this close to me was absolutely amazing. I could do this for many, many more nights. I gave her a kiss on the top of her head and soon after her breathing relaxed as she fell asleep.

Sleep wasn't coming as quickly as it did for Ciara. I keep thinking about the conversation with Millie this morning. I am wondering if she might have had a talk with Ciara. Maybe something was said that upset her. It's really hard to tell without coming right out and asking. Maybe my sleeplessness has nothing to do with Ciara's mood, maybe it's my own consciousness bothering me. I am starting to lean toward telling Ciara the truth of why she's with me. I should do that soon before I get my feelings involved deeper. I can already tell I'm falling for this amazing woman.

CHAPTER FIFTEEN
CIARA

We've been at Lincoln's home for a little over two weeks. We have done a lot of sightseeing, going on bus tours, and out to dinner every night. I've been awake for the last half hour but haven't gotten out of bed. I woke up when Lincoln got out of bed, but I felt like being lazy. I don't think he knows I woke up. I could very easily fall back to sleep as I've been fighting to stay awake.

Lincoln is the type of guy who likes to stay busy. As I said, we've done things every day since we met. I am used to staying busy myself, but with my work. This is different. I feel as if I'm on a never-ending vacation.

Little by little I am getting more comfortable around him. We have been becoming better friends than lovers at this point. We stay up all hours into the night sharing things about ourselves. Anything from childhood memories to horror stories of past relationships. We have intimate conversations, but we have not explored a sexual relationship. Yes, we've kissed many times and sleep next to one another, but nothing more has happened. I'm not sure what is holding him back from going further into our relationship. Maybe I am giving him the vibe that I am not ready for that sort of relationship yet. I haven't brought the topic up to him because I can't honestly say I'm ready for a sexual relationship with him. I'm comfortable with the way things are going. The old saying goes, slow and steady wins the race. I do care for him deeply, though.

He crawls up from the foot of the bed. His hand rubs up my spine. He kisses my cheek.

"Good morning, sleepyhead."

"Morning."

Lincoln sits lightly on the backs of my thighs. I moan when he begins to massage my shoulders. I close my eyes and enjoy what he's doing.

"I have work today. I'd love it if you came with me."

"I'm so tired."

He works his hands further down my back.

Massaging his fingers deep into my flesh. It hurts a tad but feels good at the same time. I could lay here all day having him doing this to me.

He bends forward, putting his mouth close to my ear. *"I'm meeting with Jagger and his fiancée, Oliva."*

"Shut up, you are not serious!"

"Yes I am! I planned their wedding that's happening tomorrow."

"Jagger as in Jagger Ramsey? The movie star?"

"That would be the one!"

"Are you going to this said wedding?"

"I am and so will you if you'd like to be my date."

"Will Cora and Asher be there?"

"Asher is the best man, so I would assume he'd be there."

"I'm not missing this wedding for anything."

Lincoln laughs. I try to roll over, but he keeps his weight on me and continues to massage my back. I want to see his face. He best not be messing with me.

Lincoln flips me over and pins my hands to the mattress with his. *"So are you coming with me?"*

"I think I can manage to do that."

Lincoln kisses me then gets off me and the bed. *"Better get your booty in gear, we have to leave within the hour."*

CHAPTER 15

I am so excited to go to this wedding tomorrow. I don't think Lincoln knows that I made the Santa dress that Cora wore in Stealing The Christmas Spotlight movie. I have been wanting to meet Cora ever since I saw the movie. I love how well she pulled off one of my dresses. It couldn't have fit her any better than it did.

※

Gosh, I am nervous. I shouldn't be, after all, I'm sure Asher and Cora won't be joining Jagger and Oliva when they meet with Lincoln. I don't think there'd be a reason for them to be there. I glance over to Lincoln driving. He grins and then laughs.

"Are you always this starstruck?"

"No, never. There's just something I like about Cora as a person. It helps that I like their love story."

"Asher hooked Jagger up with Oliva. Oliva is an old childhood friend of Cora's."

My eyes go wide. *"So that probably means Cora is the maid of honor?"*

"No, Cora is not in the wedding. Don't you know they split up?"

"What!? No!" He burst out laughing. I slap him. *"Don't do that, my heart can't take it."*

He can't stop laughing. I slap his upper arm again. *"I'm sorry! I won't do it again."*

We pull into the parking lot of a very large church. It's so gorgeous on the outside. My heart stops beating when I see people gathered at the door. I wasn't lying when I said I'm not ever starstruck, but meeting Cora has been on my bucket list.

"Why is everyone here?"

"You get to witness the rehearsal!"

"Oh, my, God, that's so exciting!" I literally feel like a kid on Christmas morning.

Today has been a great day. Not only did we do the rehearsal but we got invited out to lunch with everyone. It was such a pleasure getting to know not only Asher and Cora but Jagger and Olivia, as well. I learned today that Olivia will be wearing one of my designs tomorrow. I had no idea since it was bought under Olivia's mother's name. I feel so honored that she chose my dress over many others. I've only ever made a handful of wedding gowns over the years because they are a lot of work.

CHAPTER 15

After we finished with lunch, Lincoln and I came back to his home. He just poured us a couple of glasses of wine, then we came up to the rooftop of his building.

"Thank you for today. I can now mark meeting Cora off my bucket list."

"You are welcome, but I should be thanking you."

"For what? I didn't do anything."

"You did. You've done more than you know."

"What do you mean?"

"I really like you, Ciara. You are so easy to be with. I wake up every day in a better mood just by knowing I'll be with you. I watch you sleeping next to me and it fills a void I didn't know I was missing. I look forward to our conversation, your laugh, and having your hand in mine." He takes my hand in his and puts his lips to mine. *"I have to be honest with you, I'm falling for you and I didn't expect that to happen."*

I smile because I don't know what to say. I don't feel as if I can return his feelings just yet. I'm not completely sure I'm falling in love with him. I know I like him. I just don't know how far those feelings go. Our relationship has been slower than the other ones I've had. Which is fine because every relationship goes at its own pace. I do know I'd be a lucky girl if I ended up with Lincoln. He's so full of life. He's a romantic at heart. The only thing missing is the sexual chemistry that I've had with the other men. I can't put my finger on why that is. Lincoln is extremely handsome. He's downright sexy as hell. Our time together is nearly up and he has been the perfect gentleman.

"Does that scare you?"

"Sort of."

"Can you tell me why?"

"Because I've been unsure how you feel about me and our relationship until now. We haven't been intimate yet and I've been wondering why."

"It's not because I don't want you if that is what you are thinking. I've wanted to make love to you this entire time we've been together. I really want to explore that part of us, however, I've felt that you are not ready for that yet."

I take a sip of my wine and set it down. I take his other hand in mine. *"I do like you, Lincoln. You are an incredible guy. By saying that I want you to know I like our relationship and how it has developed. Sex is an important part of any relationship. You are right, I might have given you the vibe I'm not ready to explore that part of us. If I have done that I'm sorry if I have disappointed you."*

CHAPTER 15

"You haven't disappointed me in any way. If anything I might be the one disappointing you."

"That isn't possible."

"I've been keeping a secret from you. It's been nagging me every day since we met to tell you."

"I don't understand. What kind of secret?"

"I made a business deal with Millie before we ever met one another."

I let out a puff of air. *"Go on, tell me this business arrangement you have with my grandmother,"* I say, trying to hide my disappointment.

Lincoln tells me all about what he was supposed to be doing this month. For some reason, I'm not even upset.

"That is why I said I didn't expect falling for you to happen."

"I see."

"I'm really sorry for not telling you sooner. I wanted to, it's just I feared you'd leave. I'd rather have a month with you than nothing at all. You have no idea how fulfilled I feel when I'm with you. Sometimes it surprises me how quickly and easily you fit into my life."

"I'm not mad at you for not telling me. Let's forget that is why we met."

Oddly, I'm really not mad at him or Grams. I'm

more concerned about where our relationship will go from here. We only have a few days left together. I would like to see what happens over the next five days. Who knows, now that it's out in the open that we've been holding off on sexual intimacy, maybe it could happen over the next few days. If not, maybe we aren't right for one another.

CHAPTER SIXTEEN
CIARA

I am on a flight heading home two days earlier than I was supposed to be. Lincoln and I were in bed having an intimate moment when my cell phone rang. It was almost midnight. I thought about ignoring it, but something told me I needed to see who it was. When I saw it was Grams' name on the caller ID. I'm glad I didn't let it go to voicemail because it was important. I was shocked when Grams told my shop was vandalized. My first thought was about Porter. With the time difference, I didn't know if he'd still be there. She told me it must have happened moments after he left. My heart sank when she then said Porter is being questioned. I know my friend, he'd never do such a thing to me. Hell, he'd never do anything like this to a stranger or an enemy. I knew right away it wasn't him.

I frantically started getting dressed once I hung up

with Grams without explanation to Lincoln. I probably looked like a freak to him. One minute we were exploring each other's bodies and the next I jumped out of bed putting my nightclothes on. He stopped me once I started tossing my clothes in my suitcase and asked me what was going on. I told him and he got me to calm down. He got on the phone with the airlines right away while I changed into real clothes. He helped me pack once he got me on the first flight out. Within the hour we were on our way to the airport. I couldn't believe how quickly he got me on a flight home.

Saying goodbye to Lincoln the way we had to was not what either one of us expected. My emotions are already on edge from the news of my shop. I was trying my hardest to hold myself together, but having to say goodbye to him in the middle of an airport, I had a hell of a time holding my tears in. I felt Lincoln and I were finally breaking the ice and then we had to come to a sudden halt. Our relationship started out so slow and it was starting to progress in the last couple of days. We became friends before any romantic desires were acted on. Well, we were about to act on them anyway. I have had time to think on my flight and I am wondering if he and I were slower because we are better off as friends. Neither one of us said I love you. I do know he said he was falling for me, but does that mean he loves me? If he did love me, would he have told me so? I didn't say those words to him because I'm still unsure just how deep my feelings run. Could I see myself with him long term? Possibly. We built a strong friendship and most couples say they are with their best friend. I have time to figure out if Lincoln is the man for me or not.

My stomach is in knots as the driver heads toward my shop and home. I am grateful Grams had a car waiting for me when I landed. It saves me time by not having to wave down a cab. He was very helpful in getting my luggage in the trunk.

I called Grams as soon as I was on my way. She said she'd meet me there. The closer we get, the more my stomach knots. Grams didn't go into much detail, so I'm not really sure what I'll see. She did tell me the front windows have been smashed. As far as the inside goes, she didn't elaborate on it.

Within a half-hour or so the driver stops the car out front. Tears instantly fill my eyes. It isn't the broken windows that bother me. They can be replaced. It is the red spray paint on my front entrance that hurts. Whoever did this, drew a circle around my shop name then a red line through the center. Spotting a group of officers, I walk over to them and tell them who I am. When I ask to go inside, they tell me I can't until after they dust for prints and whatnot. I try my damndest to see inside, but I am pushed back toward the street by one of the officers.

By the time Grams shows up, the officers are boarding up my windows. She goes to talk to one of them then she comes to me. She has her driver get my luggage and we get in her car. She told me we are going to the police station because they are still holding Porter for questioning. I'm getting angry. First, they wouldn't allow me to step foot in my shop or go up to my apartment, they are holding my best friend. Grams tells me she'll get to the bottom of this and get Porter out of there.

Another two hours pass by before Porter is let go. We are told we still cannot go into my place. I'm exhausted, Porter and Grams are as well. We all go to Grams mansion to get some much-needed rest. It isn't until I crawl into my old bed that I text Lincoln and let him know I made it home safely and that I'm going to try and get some sleep. He didn't reply. I put my phone on charge and curl up next to my best friend and get some sleep. Although I am angry and upset, I am glad to have Porter next to me. Nothing else matters right now because the cops finally believe he had anything to do with vandalizing my shop.

I put my arm around Porter and closed my eyes. I hear my phone notify me of an incoming text message. It's probably Lincoln, but he's going to have to wait. Right now, I'm with Porter and we are tired.

CHAPTER SEVENTEEN
CIARA

I didn't sleep very well last night at all. I stayed curled up next to Porter for a few hours with my eyes wide open, then I started tossing and turning. My mind wouldn't shut off. All I could think about was who would do this to me? Why have I become a target? When is enough- enough? I have never in my life done something like this to anyone. Hell, I would never even think about doing this to another person. The only person who has ever done anything horrible to me is Bethany, Hawk's ex-assistant. She had done nothing but cause trouble since she met me. I would lay money on it that she is behind vandalizing my shop. I know I can't go around accusing people of a crime, but I sure as hell can mention to the police about her hate toward me. One thing I can't wrap my brain around is why did she and Carl sign Hawk up to date someone if she harbors feelings for him? It's not like I sought Hawk out, it was them that put him in my life.

Eventually, I did end up getting a few hours of sleep. Once I woke up, I got out of bed and left my old room so that Porter could continue to sleep without me waking him. The closer I got to the kitchen, I could smell fresh muffins being baked. My stomach rumbled, it's been since New Year's Day that smell filled my nose. Grams' cook sure does know how to bake. I enter the kitchen and Grams is sitting in her usual place. We say good morning to one another as I join her. Right away a hot cup of tea is placed in front of me with a muffin. I reach for the butter and my stomach growls. I giggle as Grams smiles and shakes her head.

"Did you get any sleep? You look tired."

"Not very much," I tell her. *"I think it was almost eight before I stopped tossing and turning."*

"I didn't get much myself."

"Have you heard from anyone yet?"

"I just got off the phone with the police. They are still going over surveillance footage from the other stores. Yours showed nothing of use. The people kept their heads down so their faces weren't shown on camera. Since none of the other storefronts were touched, this was directly targeting you."

"I think I might have an idea of who this could have been behind this. Although, I didn't realize it was more than one person. I do however think it is the same person behind the tabloids."

"You know who is feeding the tabloids?"

"I do. It's Bethany."

"Bethany who?"

"Hawk Evans assistant. Well, she isn't that anymore because he fired her."

"Everything did start about that time. I'll let the authorities know. Go ahead and get that muffin or two in your belly."

Even though this muffin smells amazing and I have it all buttered up, I am not sure I can stomach it. There is no way Grams won't let me get away without eating after she heard the growling noise it made. I sit here and choke it down while she gets on the phone with the police. I don't want to be right, but I hope I am. She has been a royal pain in my ass and she needs to be stopped so that I can stop worrying about her.

CHAPTER 17

When Grams got off the phone, she told me we can go into my shop, so I went and woke Porter up. When I picked up my phone, I saw that I had multiple messages from all the guys, except from Hawk. I read them all on the way to my place and replied to them. They all showed their concern for me. I told them that I was fine and that I haven't been able to go inside yet to see the damage. It showed me how much each one of them cared for my wellbeing. I am fine, I just want whoever has done this to me to stop.

Arriving at my shop, my nerves are on edge. There are people gathered outside on the sidewalk taking pictures. A part of me doesn't want to see what the inside looks like. Grams tells me whatever the damage is, she'll fix it. I take little comfort in that. It shouldn't need to be fixed. I see the boarded-up windows and I feel sick to my stomach. Someone wrote *bitch* in spray paint. Whoever did this came back? Probably waited until the police left. To me, that means they were lurking in the background waiting for an opportunity to make their presence known.

Grams driver pushed his way through the gathered crowd to get us inside. My heart sinks when we get inside. My shop is destroyed. All my designs are cut to shreds. I don't think they left one piece of clothing alone.

"Holy shit!"

Grams, Porter, and I all turn around at the same time. He lifts his sunglasses and takes off his baseball cap. *"Hawk?"*

"Who did this?"

I am in too much shock to see him standing in my messed up shop to answer him. Grams crosses her arms over her chest, almost in disgust. I find my voice before she gives him the third degree.

"We are not sure yet. I was thinking maybe Bethany."

"That can't be."

Now I cross my arms over my chest. *"Why do you think it wasn't her?"*

"Because she is heading Upstate to a track with a driver."

"How do you know that?"

"She started dating him three weeks ago. If you notice she stopped feeding the tabloids."

"Oh! I didn't notice. I try not to pay attention to them."

Grams and Porter make themselves scarce, giving Hawk and me a minute alone. He comes toward me and I just stare at him. Damn, he's sexy as hell with his shaggy haircut.

"You look amazing as ever."

"What are you doing here?"

"Race is at a road course track Upstate. I saw the paper this morning and thought I'd swing by on my way through."

"I thought you were out of racing for a while?"

"I am, but I still show up to support my substitute. I'm actually getting back in the car next weekend."

"That's great!"

"I can't wait."

"Are you scared to wreck again?"

"Not really. I think I'll be more cautious, but not scared."

Hawk leans against the counter. He then grabs me by the waist and pulls me toward him. I wrap my arms around his neck and hug him. I forgot how great he smells.

"I feel bad that my first thought was Bethany did this to my store."

"Don't, she hasn't made your life very easy since meeting her."

"I seriously don't know who else would have done this to me."

"By the writing on the wall, whoever it was, said it's karma."

I turn around and look to where Hawk is looking. In big red letters is spray painted karma on the far wall. I had not noticed it since I was so in shock over what they did to my clothes.

"I don't understand. I haven't done anything to anyone to deserve this."

"I know. I'm sorry this happened to you. I am sure whoever did this is an asshole and a very jealous one." His hands cup my face. *"I have really missed you."* Before I can reply, his lips are on mine. My feelings for him come rushing back. I remember everything we have done for and with one another. I shouldn't have been so shocked he showed up here, Hawk is very spontaneous.

Grams comes out from the backroom and starts poking around in the torn up clothing. Hawk leaned into my ear and whispered that he needs to go because Carl is waiting for him out in the car. He gives me another kiss - a longer, deeper kiss. My daredevil didn't care that he is breaking Grams rules right in front of her. I smile inside, knowing I like it. We said goodbye and I watched him put his shades and ball cap back on, then went out the door.

I tell Grams it couldn't have been Bethany once

he is gone. She said she figured that out. She told me to follow her up to my apartment. We go out the back way because of the crowd. When we get to my door, more words are written, but this time in permanent marker that says, "Bitch this has just begun. You will be sorry we ever met."

Fear fills me instantly. Someone is after me and I have no idea why. I can't think of one person who I mistreated to have an enemy such as this one.

ABOUT THE AUTHOR

Thank you so much for taking the time to read Grandma's Silent Auction - June. Word-of-mouth is crucial for any author to succeed. If you enjoyed the book, please leave a review on Amazon. Even if it's just a sentence or two. It would make all the difference and would be very much appreciated. – OXOX Michael James

Michael's Links:

Website: http://michaeljames-author332.bravesites.com/

ALSO BY MICHAEL JAMES

If you enjoyed Grandma's Secret Auction, you may also like my other books:

The Way We Love series:

Pink Skies At Night

Shadows At Night

Nights Are Unlimited

Concealed By The Night

Shattered At Night

Freed At Night

Winning A Cowgirl's Heart - Trilogy:

The Rodeo King

The Best Friend

The Fate Of My Heart

Winning a Cowgirl's Heart -Complete Box Set

Construction Vs. Corporate- Trilogy:

Unbalanced

Balancing

Balanced

Secrets Within a Club

Club Comrade

Revenge

Saving Club Conrad

Masquerade Saga

His Pearls

His Secrets

His Prison

His Games

His Moves

All His

Crime in Landkaster series

The Mirror

Times Like These

Lonely Road of Faith

Grandma's Silent Auction series

January

February

March

April

May

Lost Love Letter

I'll be Waiting

Standalone:

Toying With October

Pieces Of Me

A Christmas For Eve

Dom Diaries: Tangled Up In You

Christmas Scavenger Hunt

Blue Christmas

Stealing the Christmas Spotlight

Co-written with Jodi Fahey

Last Sheet

Co-written with Daniel Grayson

Inside the Storm

Made in United States
Cleveland, OH
06 April 2025